# PENNY PL

## *a Pumpkin*

# KATIE HEDRICK

*For Grandpa Jim, who taught me all the life lessons that come with growing things.*

*For Grandma Lori, who is patient and kind. Thank you for the way you loved Grandpa and the way you love our family.*

*1 Corinthians 13:4*

It was the last day of school at Poppy Public School on Pleasant Hill.

"The summer fun possibilities are endless!" Penny the Peculiar Penguin proclaimed to her friends Polly the Parrot and Peggy the Platypus.

"I'm going to make purple popsicles and visit a petting zoo," said Polly.

"My family plans to have fun at Palm Tree Waterpark," Peggy explained with excitement.

Penny smiled. "Those sound like perfect options! My family is going to plant a garden. I'm hoping to enter the Plumpest Pumpkin Contest when it takes place in the fall," Penny said.

"That's going to take a lot of patience," said Polly. "Fall is a long time away. You'll have to wait all summer before the Plumpest Pumpkin Contest takes place!"

"That is a long period of time," Penny pondered out loud, "but I'm pretty certain I can handle the waiting part."

The three friends parted ways and Penny proceeded home.

Later that evening Penny smelled something pleasant. She poked her head into the kitchen to see her mama and papa flipping pancakes.

"It's breakfast for supper tonight. Papa is making his special peach pancakes," Mama said.

"Peach pancakes are positively delicious!" Penny piped up.

Papa poured some syrup on the peach pancakes. "Since tomorrow is the first day of summer break, we will plan to plant the garden."

"Super!" Penny exclaimed.

Penny couldn't wait to plant the entire garden, but she was particularly excited about the thought of growing a prize winning pumpkin.

"Grandpa and Grandma are coming to help too," Papa said.

Early the next morning when the sun was peeking over the horizon with streams of purple and gold, Grandpa and Grandma pulled up in their pickup. Penny thought it felt like the perfect day to plant a prize winning pumpkin.

Papa began to plow the dirt.

Grandpa put his flipper around Penny. "It's important to tend to the soil in which you are growing things," he said. "If we provide a proper environment, then the seeds we plant will grow and prosper."

"We are ready to plant," Papa stated.

The penguin family began poking holes in the dirt. Then they dropped in tiny seeds. There were potatoes, parsnips, peppers and parsley. Mama even planted a row of purple petunias.

Finally, it was time for Penny to plant her pumpkin seed. Grandpa watched proudly as Penny carefully placed her pumpkin seed in the dirt, patted it and sprinkled water on top.

"Now comes the hard part," Grandpa explained. "It's time to be patient, and eventually you will reap what you have sown, Penny."

The penguin family celebrated the completion of the garden planting with Grandma's famous pecan pie.

Later as Grandpa and Grandma loaded up in the pickup Grandpa offered one more piece of advice.

"Be sure to protect the seeds you planted, Penny. Pull out any pesky weeds that would prevent your plants from growing."

Penny appreciated the wisdom Grandpa shared. Year after year, he and Grandma would plant the crops at their farm, always taking particular care to ensure a plentiful harvest.

Penny couldn't wait for her pumpkin plant to grow. She did everything she could think of to pass the time.

She practiced piano, played with Play-Doh, painted pictures and pretended to be pirates with her siblings. Penny even performed a play for her mama and papa.

Being patient was hard. Penny pondered the possibility that perhaps her pumpkin seed would never sprout.

A few days later Penny popped out to the garden to take a peek. To her pleasant surprise, a tiny green plant was poking out of the soil. It was her pumpkin!

As the summer proceeded on, Penny took particularly good care of her pumpkin plant.

She provided it a proper environment with water and fertilizer. She protected it by pulling out the pesky weeds that popped up. Most importantly, she practiced patience because Grandpa had promised that in due time she would reap what she had sown.

Penny's plant flourished and it grew into a perfectly round and plump pumpkin!

Finally the day of the Plumpest Pumpkin Contest arrived. Penny's family and friends gathered at Pinecone Park.

Penny felt positively excited, yet a little apprehensive.

Mayor Pam the Opossum stood near the playground and projected through a megaphone, "May I have your attention please! It's time for the pumpkin judging! Proceed to the picnic table with your pumpkins."

Penny picked up her pumpkin and placed it in the judging area. She spotted pumpkins of all shapes and sizes.

Piper the Porcupine had grown a pink pumpkin. Phil the Pig's pumpkin was prickly and pear shaped. Poncho the Parakeet's pumpkin looked approximately the same size as Penny's, but it was peach in color.

Mayor Pam padded along, patting each of the pumpkins. At last she proclaimed, "I'm pleased to award the purple ribbon prize to Penny! She has grown this year's plumpest pumpkin!"

The crowd applauded as Penny placed the purple ribbon on her pumpkin.

Grandpa smiled proudly at Penny and nodded in approval. Penny's patience had paid off and just like Grandpa said, she reaped what had been sown.

To everything there is a season,
A time for every purpose under heaven.

(ECCLESIASTES 3:1 NEW KING JAMES VERSION)


Be anxious for nothing, but in everything by prayer and supplication, with thanksgiving, let your requests be made known to God.

(PHILIPPIANS 4:6 NEW KING JAMES VERSION)


And let us not grow weary while doing good, for in due season we shall reap if we do not lose heart.

(GALATIANS 6:9 NEW KING JAMES VERSION)

Made in the USA
Middletown, DE
28 February 2022

61916188R00015